A FIELD GUIDE TO HIGH SCHOOL

This book is a gift from:

Kitty Arenz

EDITED BY MARISSA WALSH

Not Like I'm Jealous or Anything: The Jealousy Book

A FIELD GUIDE TO HIGH SCHOOL

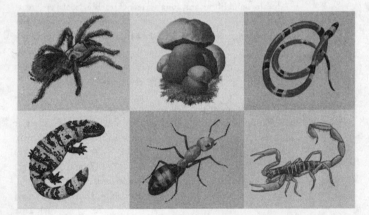

A NOVEL BY MARISSA WALSH

DELACORTE PRESS

Published by Delacorte Press
an imprint of Random House Children's Books
a division of Random House, Inc.
New York

Delacorte Press and colophon are registered trademarks of Random House, Inc.
Visit us on the Web! www.randomhouse.com/teens
Educators and librarians, for a variety of teaching tools, visit us at
www.randomhouse.com/teachers

The Library of Congress has cataloged the hardcover edition of this work
as follows:
Walsh, Marissa.
A field guide to high school / Marissa Walsh.
p. cm.
Summary: Andie and her best friend Bess read through a manual Andie's Yale-
bound sister wrote for her, which is filled with tips and tricks for excelling at
Plumstead Country Day high school where Andie is about to be a freshman.
ISBN 978-0-385-73410-3 (hardcover)
ISBN 978-0-385-90427-8 (Gibraltar lib. bdg.)
[1. High schools—Fiction. 2. Interpersonal relations—Fiction.
3. Sisters—Fiction. 4. Humorous stories.]
I. Title
PZ7.W16865Fie 2007
[Fic]—dc22
2006028108

ISBN 978-0-385-73411-0 (tr. pbk.)
Printed in the United States of America
10 9 8 7 6 5 4 3 2 1
First Trade Paperback Edition

To my high school teachers

He had to tell Goober to play ball, to play
football, to run, to make the team, to sell the
chocolates, to sell whatever they wanted you to
sell, to do whatever they wanted you to do.

—Jerry, *The Chocolate War*

Uh, this is high school. We're here for four years
and then we move on. And all these people you see
every day vanish from your life and you never have
to think about them again.

—Veronica, *Veronica Mars*

The day my older sister, Claire, left for college she gave me this book.

This is how it happened. When I went outside to get in the car that would bring Claire and her stuff to college, there was a minifridge in my seat. And it wasn't moving. "It's either it or me," I said. My parents looked at each other. My mother gave me money for pizza and said they wouldn't be home too too late. My father gave me a weak smile. As they pulled away, Claire smirked out the window, then made that stupid Macaulay Culkin *Home Alone* face at me: a hand on each cheek and her mouth opened wide. I gave her the finger. Then I went back inside—there was no reason to start the day at this ungodly hour. Claire was the crazy one who had insisted on leaving at five-thirty a.m. because she wanted to beat her roommate there so she could get the best side. "Everyone knows that's how it works," she had explained. I didn't think that was the nicest way to start things off, but I didn't say anything. You couldn't argue with Claire.

She had signed up for some pre-pre-preorientation college thing so she could "survey the competition, get a jump on everyone else, and hit the ground running." Part of her motivation for doing this was because she had, according to her, been given the worst incoming first-year student at Yale for a roommate. Someone who had probably only applied there because she wanted to be like Rory on *Gilmore Girls*. Or First Daughter Barbara Bush. I didn't think being like Rory was such a bad thing, but I kept my mouth shut. Besides, I secretly thought it was possible Claire had chosen Yale for the same reason.

What had happened was, my sister had sent the nice, summertime hello-I-like-to-sleep-with-the-window-open friendly e-mail to her roommate and received no response. My sister was not used to receiving no response. This was not how one treated my sister.

That girl was toast.

And so was I.

Claire had been like Ms. Plumstead Country Day, which was the stupid name of the stupid high school I'd be going to and she had just graduated from. She was popular, captain of the field hockey team, pretty, and smart. Yes, she was a total high school cliché. They should have shipped her out to Laguna Beach. And now she was going to Yale, where she would probably become a total college cliché. And I was starting at Plumstead, pretty sure no one would ever be crowning me anything except "Claire Petersen's little (maybe she's adopted?) sister."

I hadn't wanted to go to Plumstead. Claire and I had always gone to public school, but then when it was time for Claire to go to high school she was recruited by Plumstead, and for some reason I still don't understand my parents agreed to send her there.

It had never occurred to me that I would have to go there, too. I just assumed I would go to the public high school, or to Pope Mother Teresa XXXIII, the Catholic school my best friend, Bess, was going to. But I didn't even get a choice. As usual, I was paying the price of being related to Claire.

Plumstead hadn't recruited me—they were just stuck with *me* because I was related to *her*. I wasn't a star like Claire. I got Bs. I was good at soccer but I wasn't the captain. I never scored. If Bess were here she would point out that that's because I played defense, which is true. But it is also true that I am just average. My big sister is the most interesting thing about me.

As I jumped back into bed, my knee hit something hard. I reached under my blanket: it was a book. But it wasn't mine and it hadn't been there when I'd gotten up. *Claire.* Either she had forgotten it or it was an overdue library book she wanted me to return for her. Typical.

My cell phone rang. It was five-forty-five. Who would be calling?

"Did you find it?"

"What?"

"The book I left for you?"

"Who is this?"

Claire snorted. "Oh, so you've forgotten me already?"

I started to hang up.

"Wait! Andie! Are you in my room?"

* * *

4

I tried to go back to sleep but the book taunted me from the floor. It was as if Claire had never left. And with the new family-plan cell phones she had insisted my parents invest in for college (playing the safety card really works, by the way), she would continue to call me until I had read it and given her an A+. It was either that or change my number.

To be honest, I had nothing better to do. I opened the book, which Claire had modestly titled "A Field Guide to High School." It looked like she had found an actual old field guide at a used-book store—this one was about poisonous plants and venomous animals—except that she had pasted over the descriptions of poison oak and scorpions. It was one of those Peterson's guides, which was mildly amusing, because our last name just happens to be Petersen, with an "e." I guess there *was* a reason my sister had gotten into Yale—she could be clever when she wanted to be.

I needed reinforcements. It was a bit early, but this was an emergency. And I knew that Bess slept with her cell phone.

"I hate you."

"Bess, you *must* get over here."

"What? Andie, it's six a.m. I thought you went to Yale."

"It's a long story."

She grumbled something about an hour and hung up.

I felt a little guilty involving Bess, but she was my best friend. We shared everything. If Claire was going to pass down some secret information about high school, I wanted Bess to know about it, too. Plus, I knew she didn't have anything better to do. The only thing was, Bess didn't like Claire. She thought Claire was a fake, annoying, rah-rah preppy person. And I can't defend Claire—she was that. But she was also my sister. I knew her in a different way. She hadn't always been like this.

I think Claire could tell that Bess wasn't a fan. It obviously would have been easier for me if my best friend and my sister got along. But it was also helpful to have Bess in my corner, all to myself. Claire could do no wrong, in my parents' eyes. They hadn't been able to see anything except her four-year-long getting-into-college campaign.

The doorbell rang.

Bess's hair was wet.

"I can't believe my sister!"

She took the book out of my hands.

"Oh, I can. So you just found this on your bed?"

"Yes. There was no room in the car, and my parents didn't even try to fit me, and then I went back to bed and there it was."

"She must have planned it. She wanted you to read it instead of coming. She probably didn't want to have to introduce you to her new Yale friends." Bess was paging through the book. "Do you have any cereal?"

"Bess!"

"What? I'm hungry. You didn't give me time for breakfast."

She started rifling through cabinets. "Kashi? Grape-Nuts? Total? Don't you have any sugar cereal?"

"Have you not been here before? You know what we have."

She got herself a bowl and filled it with Total.

"You know what? I've been thinking." She took a bite. "And this is what I've decided: your sister is a bitch."

This is why Bess is my best friend. She isn't afraid to tell it like it is.

"How could she just hand this to you and leave? I mean, a field guide to high school? Is she kidding? She knows you don't even want to go to that stupid school. Doesn't she? Is she just trying to rub it in?"

I don't think she was. I think in her weird, twisted overachiever way, my sister was actually trying to help. To be nice. Of course, she had been too busy all summer to actually sit down and just talk to me in person about what to expect. She was never home to answer my questions, and she was so obsessed with buying herself the right college wardrobe and room accessories that she hadn't had time to help me with mine. I mean, didn't *I* deserve a new wardrobe, too? Isn't starting high school just as important as starting college?

But I didn't say anything. Bess didn't have these problems. She was an only child. And she was going to a Catholic high school. With uniforms! I wanted to go there with her, because I wanted to be at the same school, but truthfully, I was happy I wasn't going to have to wear a uniform. There's something to be said for personal expression. Even in high school.

Bess broke the silence. "When are your parents coming home?"

"Late. They gave me pizza money."

"Guess we'll just have to add another book to our required summer reading list."

A Field
Guide
to High
School

Andie,

After four years of high school, I have graduated. And graduated well, I might add. How did I do this? By being *constantly* aware of my surroundings. By keeping my friends close and my enemies closer. By striking first. By knowing what *not* to wear.

Thanks to Mom and Dad's poor planning and neurotic loyalty to Dr. Spock (the baby doctor, not the *Star Trek* guy), there are four years between us. Four years. The difference between College Freshman and High School Not-So-Fresh-Feeling Person. My journey is over; yours is just beginning. And sadly, I won't be there to play Virgil to your Dante, Alicia Silverstone's Cher to your Brittany Murphy's Tai. You're going to have to make it in high school on your own. At least you'll have Mom and Dad's full attention (when they're not too busy missing me), not to mention the bathroom to yourself.

You might think that the best way to prepare for high school is to watch all the high school movies you can find. That would be a bad idea. High school is not a movie. Or a TV show, for that matter. In high school the kids are actually the age they should be, unlike on *That '70s Show* or *Beverly Hills, 90210*, where the actors are already in their twenties. Also, a bad or annoying kid might show up on *one* episode of those shows, but in real life he is not dealt with and shown the error of his ways and banished forever at the end of the hour. Oh, no—in real life, he will continue to sit behind you in class for the next four years because his father is one of the science teachers. Or a trustee.

Just be grateful Mom and Dad didn't make you go to boarding school. (They told me once they were thinking about it.) And don't play dumb—I know you stole my copy of *Prep*.

According to the original author of this field guide, "This book is designed to help you keep out of trouble in the field." I couldn't have said it better myself.

Good luck, And. You're going to need it.

xo

Claire

P.S. This isn't technically a real field guide. A real field guide would be boring.

Bess looked up. "Ha! We'll be the judge of that."

part one
POISONOUS PLANTS

Lots of plants and flowers look nice, but if
you eat them it's another story.
These are the things they don't tell you.

THE KEY TO FAKING OUT THE PARENTS IS THE
CLAMMY HANDS. IT'S A GOOD NONSPECIFIC SYMP-
TOM; I'M A BIG BELIEVER IN IT. . . . YOU FAKE A
STOMACH CRAMP, AND WHEN YOU'RE BENT OVER,
MOANING AND WAILING, YOU LICK YOUR PALMS. IT'S
A LITTLE CHILDISH AND STUPID, BUT THEN, SO IS
HIGH SCHOOL.   —FERRIS, *Ferris Bueller's Day Off*

"What is it with your sister and this movie?"
"I don't know! She was obsessed."

UMBRELLALIKE CLUSTERS; LEAVES FINELY DIVIDED [ORIENTATION]

Orientation is just one of the things that distinguish private school from public. And you might think it's one of the things that are cool or special about going to private school, that make it feel more like college. Well, don't. Don't be taken in by it. Orientation is a waste of time. It's also at a fake-Indian-sounding place called Camp Chewonkee.

In public school, they don't try to mess with the social order. They know they can't change it, so they just let it be. In private school, they think they can get involved, and they impose things like orientation—which means silly get-to-know-each-other games and exercises—on you. Apparently you can't begin private school without throwing a ball at someone while yelling their name, and/or falling backward into twelve outstretched arms. You will have to repeat your name and where you are from many times, so start practicing now. Come up with a fun backstory for yourself. But not too fun. If you have to talk about what you did on your summer vacation, say you were rebuilding New Orleans. Or traveling. You don't have to be specific. If they ask where, just say "the Continent." Whatever you do, *don't* tell them you worked at the library. Not if you want a prom date.

Don't wear a new "back-to-school" outfit to orientation. You will stick out. And don't wait for the school to tell you this, or anything, because they never will. That's what I'm here for.

At orientation you will need to be able to move, and it will be hot, Indian summer, and you will be too warm in your sweater and long-sleeved shirt. The other private-school kids will know this, because they've already been through orientations. Wearing the wrong thing could be your first, fatal mistake. Save the fall clothes for the end of the month or October.

For orientation and beyond, looking like you don't care is the way to go. It's best not to try too hard. Or, better yet, to not *look* like you tried too hard. In high school you never want to look like you tried too hard, at anything. Never let anyone see you sweat. Make it look easy. Your seams should never be visible.

I made that mistake at my orientation. I wore a new back-to-school fall outfit. Not just clothes—an outfit. But orientation was on a wet field, and it was early enough in September that it was hot, and I was boiling. All the kids were checking each other out, sizing each other up, and it might have been warm but the group was cold. And then we had to do these annoying trust exercises with people we had never met before. And in sixth grade we'd have all thought it looked cool, but now people were rolling their eyes and no one wanted to be there. I had wanted to go, so I just assumed they had, too. I mean, had they ever been to public school? There was no such thing as orientation in public school. School just started. You weren't given a day to just hang out and have fun.

Orientation is the first opportunity for everyone—your fellow freshmen—to try to figure out who is cool. And in your world, the only people who matter are your fellow freshmen. They will judge a book by its cover. You'll do it, too. And that is the hardest thing about being fourteen and starting over someplace where you don't know anybody. People form a superficial opinion of you, and once it's out there it's virtually impossible to overcome. It sucks, but that's the way it is. Lots of things about the next four years get decided at orientation. So be careful about how you present yourself. In high school, you rarely, if ever, get a second chance to make a first impression. By the first day of school, things will already be in place. It will be hard to go back and fix whatever damage you've caused.

Oh, and when orientation's over, after the trust has been built, everyone will retreat to their preestablished groups and orientation will be memorable only because it was the first and last time some of your classmates ever spoke to you.

Bess looked at me. "If you make a new best friend at Plumstead *I'll* kill *you*!"

I laughed. "Well, if you make a new best friend at Mother Teresa I'll kill you!"

"Okay. That's settled."

"Are you sure? You don't need a pinky swear?"

Bess pouted. "I'm sure."

MISCELLANEOUS FLOWERS; MOSTLY SHOWY
[GETTING THERE, IN ORDER OF COOLNESS]

School starts the minute you leave the house in the morning, whether you take the bus, drive, or walk. You must be *on*. Some girls think it's cool to show up disheveled, with wet hair, sipping their coffee. Obviously I am not one of them.

And the importance of *how* you get to school is not to be underestimated. Socially, it can make or break you.

CARPOOL, STUDENT DRIVER: Your social class can really be influenced by who you ride with. If it's a cool person, some of her cool will rub off on you just from being seen with her for the one minute it takes to drive from the school gate to the student parking lot. That minute is crucial. Carpool might be the only time you will ever speak to or interact with an upperclassman. And if that upperclassman is nice, she will take you under her wing. If that upperclassman is not nice, she will take your gas money but never acknowledge you during the school day, except when she is going to leave early and has to break the news to you that you will have to find your own way home. Some of the fun carpools stop at Dunkin' Donuts in the morning and all seem to like each other.

Riding with another student is also preferable because it places you in the student parking lot in the morning, which is the place to see and be seen, especially by the always-elusive upperclassmen. And you get to walk into school from the parking lot, which is the best way to arrive. If you are a freshman or a sophomore, this signals that you are a cut above.

DRIVE SELF: Then you have the kids who drive themselves to school in their own car, which is ten times better than our—and the faculty's—cars. It's not as cool if the driver is alone, unless the car is unusually cool and it's about making a statement. The girl with the vintage pink Karmann Ghia, for example. She probably doesn't want passengers! But there are some boys who drive alone and you get the feeling that no parents wanted their kids riding with them. Or conversely, some parents (lawyers, usually) who didn't want their kids driving anybody else, for legal reasons. You can never be too careful.

BUS: If there is a large-enough concentration of kids in a few different neighboring towns, the school will sponsor a bus. For a price, of course. It's not cool to take the bus, but it's not as bad as being driven by a parent or other adult. There are antics, naturally, on the bus, as there always are, so some of those kids will become friends and have their bus connection. Most kids only take the bus for the first year or two, then either drive themselves or find a carpool.

CAR WITH CHAUFFEUR: School legend has it that there was once a boy who was driven to school not by a parent or another student but by a professional driver who was part of his family's household staff. I have not been able to confirm this.

CARPOOL, ADULT DRIVER: There are different kinds of carpools. Most of them are based on where people live, and that's how people refer to them, by town name. The [insert town] carpool. Again, that one minute from the school gate to the front of the school is crucial, and even though everyone in the student parking lot will see you—that can't be avoided—it's best to get dropped off some distance away from the front door so *those* people don't see Mom and Dad's bad car, or so that at least there will be enough cars coming and going that it might not be obvious which one is ours. Naturally, this plan works best if you can keep Mom from beeping and waving after she drops you off.

One problem with the carpool is that you move as one. If one person has to stay late for some reason and their parent is driving that day, then you all have to stay late. Unless you get your own ride. If you are late in the morning, your whole carpool is late. And it will be your fault. They won't forget it.

There are a few kids whose parents teach at Plumstead. I assume they just ride to school with the parent who works there. I suppose if you go to the school where your parent is a teacher you've got bigger things to worry about than being seen in a car with them.

You sometimes catch a glimpse of the teachers arriving in the morning, in their uncool cars, probably with tape decks, listening to NPR.

WALK: The roads around Plumstead have no sidewalks, so it isn't exactly easy to walk. There are a few kids who live close enough, however. The headmaster actually lives in a house on campus, as does his son, who is a student. But I've never seen the son walking to school from the house. He must time it so that he leaves before anyone else arrives or after everyone gets there, but not so that he'll be late. Come to think of it, I've also never seen him with his father. Ever. He must be good at keeping a low profile by now.

KID WITHOUT A CARPOOL: There are always a few kids no one wants to drive. They are just too weird or chatty or they smell. It's not even worth the gas money to have them in your car. There was one girl whose carpool would always leave early, without her, but her parents refused to come pick her up. They made her find her own ride home. It was cruel. Everyone avoided her at the end of the day.

NOTE: Every so often the local police decide they are going to crack down on students speeding on the road that leads up to the school. One day a girl who lived right down the street was pulled over directly in front of the school gate. Everyone—including the teachers—saw her. It was the talk of morning meeting. All the boys called her a badass.

"I didn't realize getting to school was such an issue."
"It seems like everything with your sister is an issue."
"It didn't used to be. In elementary school we took the bus. In junior high, Dad dropped me off on his way to work."
"Didn't Claire get a ride to Plumstead with that weird kid?"

"Yes! Max Fisher. Mom and Dad made her. She was so mean to him."

"At least he had a nice car."

"Yeah, and he's at MIT."

DEATH CAMAS: SIX-PARTED STARS IN RACEMES OR PANICLES
[THE FIRST DAY OF SCHOOL]

Remember when we were little and the first day of school was exciting and you couldn't sleep the night before and you couldn't eat breakfast because of the butterflies? Well, it's the same thing now, but for different reasons.

I nudged Bess. "Remember the first day of school last year?"

"What about it?"

"It was so nice to finally be in eighth grade. We were on top—everyone else was below us. I don't want to start all over."

Bess shrugged. "We don't have a choice."

On the first day of school, the sophomores, juniors, and seniors will be boisterous. Lots of them have been away for the summer and are seeing their friends for the first time since last school year. The senior boys will be checking you out. Everyone will be jockeying for power and figuring out what their new roles are and how they are going to be. Even the teachers, the headmaster, and the chef are trying to make a good impression. (The food that first week is always the best.) They know you can always transfer schools or change classes around if you are unhappy.

Most of the other ninth graders will be walking around just as clueless as you are. Just remember that everyone is new, even if some of them already know each other.

It's a small window, though, so you must take advantage of it now. In a few weeks, the die will be cast. And you're either in or out. Sometimes it's necessary to strike first.

WHAT NOT TO DO:

1. Don't dress up too much. This is high school, not second grade. In high school, everyone notices if you show up with a brand-new outfit and new shoes. It's best not to come on too strong. It's fine to get ideas from magazines, but never be obvious about it. Like, don't actually wear the entire outfit shown in the back-to-school issue of *Teen Vogue.*

It's fine to sneak in a few pieces from Old Navy, H&M, or the Gap, but never buy anything with patterns or logos that identify the piece as actually being from Old Navy, H&M, or the Gap. You might want to keep an extra outfit in your gym locker in case you ever show up wearing exactly the same thing as someone else.

But you don't want to stand out, either. The trick is to wear clothes that are close to what everyone else is wearing while not actually being the exact same clothes. Got it?

2. Don't let Mom and Dad take a picture. Or get out of the car. Better yet, get to school before anyone else on the first day so no one sees how you got there. Create an air of mystery around yourself.

3. Don't ask for help from an upperclassman. There are two reasons for this: 1. You don't want to show your hand. If an upperclassman senses that you are weak, they will take advantage of it. You want to act as if you have been going to the school for two years, not two hours. 2. Most upperclassmen can't be trusted. They might give you false information. Remember, they are threatened by your arrival.

4. Don't introduce yourself as my sister. No one likes a show-off. And believe me, you're better off *not* bringing comparisons between us upon yourself.

5. Don't wear any of my old clothes. Self explanatory: people might recognize them and know you are wearing hand-me-downs. Or think that you have raided my closet in my absence.

6. Don't answer any questions in class. We all know you're smart but you don't want to be labeled a teacher's pet or a show-off in the first week,

especially if you are in classes with upperclass-men. They will feel like you are showing them up, feel stupid, and take it out on you. Remember, in marathons as in life, slow but steady wins the race.

7. Don't try to sit at an upperclassman lunch table. Off-limits. Freshmen sit with freshmen.

8. Don't spill your lunch tray all over the head-master or do anything that is going to peg you for the entire year as "the girl who spilled her lunch on the headmaster." High school students are like elephants. They never forget. Unless you give them something even more memorable to remember.

NOTE: In general, if people mention something you don't know anything about, just nod and smile. Then move on. Pretty soon they will just assume you are deaf and stop talking to you.

Bess started laughing and couldn't stop.

I rolled my eyes at her. "I don't want people to think I'm deaf."

"Does Plumstead have a Sign Language Club?"

"You despise Claire, remember? But you're just as bad as she is."

"Even you have to admit that this stuff is

pretty funny. I love the part about spilling your tray on the headmaster!"

"You know, I think that might have actually happened. Are you getting the feeling Claire rigged up a camera in her closet so I wouldn't take anything?"

"Hey, if she didn't bring it to college with her then it's fair game until Thanksgiving."

"And of course I'm going to raise my hand in class if I know the answer. That's ridiculous. Claire may not have to worry about college anymore but I still do!"

POISON OAK
[BUILDING AND GROUNDS]

Familiarize yourself with your surroundings. Plumstead has an art room, a dance studio, a billiards room. It's like Clue. You'd never find most of these things in public school. But don't let on that you know that.

When you're a freshman, there are some places that aren't accessible to you—certain lunch tables, Senior Slope (the hill behind the school that gets the best sun)—so don't even think about it. Mistakes are not tolerated. You've been warned.

ART GALLERY: It's cool that you attend a school with an art gallery, but never admit that or actually be seen looking at the art. Maybe after hours when there's no one else around you can sneak a peek, but that's it. And if you have a piece of art hanging there, pretend you don't know anything about it or how it got there.

ART ROOM: High school artists tend to come from the leftover group—often skaters and goths. In other words, the nonpopular people. So the art room, where these people call home, is not a place for you. The art teacher tends to be—how shall I say it?—subversive. She encourages individual expression. But everyone who's anyone knows that individual expression will not make you popular.

BALCONIES: A few of the rooms have windowed doors that open onto small wrought-iron balconies that have seen better days. Seriously. I don't recommend stepping outside on them. Señora Froot Loop thought otherwise and during a particularly exhilarating AP Spanish class decided she needed *un momento*. Four of us formed a human chain to pull her back in after the thing started to shake. (Señora likes her guacamole.)

BOILER ROOM: There's a basement shortcut from the gym to the cafeteria through the boiler room that some skaters and goths use, even though we're not really supposed to. I don't like it—it's dark and scary and there are pipes and it always sounds as if the boiler is about to blow. If you absolutely have to go through there I suggest moving as quickly as possible. It's known as a make-out spot during dances, but there have also been unsubstantiated sightings of creatures that sound suspiciously similar to those encountered by Harry Potter and his little friends.

BOOK LOCKERS: In private school, the kids leave their bags piled in the hallways. That's a big thing to adjust to—the realization that no one is going to steal your bag or open or vandalize it. The worst that will happen is that your bag will look like everyone else's and you won't be able to figure out which one is yours. (Another reason for a handy L.L.Bean monogram!) It's important for you to start internalizing now that private school is not like public school, where if you leave your locker door open for one second to run to catch someone you can kiss its entire contents goodbye, including your irreplaceable picture of the shirtless Abercrombie boy, which will be shredded and littered all over the hallway.

At Plumstead, no one uses a lock on their book locker. So don't betray yourself as a public-school kid by putting a lock on yours. There was one tough kid with a chip on his shoulder who put one on once. It made people uncomfortable. He stuck out. And he got in trouble—he had to go see the dean of students about it.

Not to say that private school is Utopia. There was an incident. Once. It was sad and scary and involved a girl who was a klepto. The school actually had to set a trap. Exploding dye was involved. But don't mention it because we're not supposed to talk about it. The girl was expelled and everyone feels safe again now.

High school kids don't decorate their lockers. Most people don't even keep their books there—they carry them around in their book bag. The cool seniors only carry one book at a time and return to their lockers between classes to switch books. They are never seen carrying their bags during school. They are never seen rifling through the piles trying to find theirs after lunch. They saunter through the halls without a care in the world, oblivious to the bells, books tucked perfectly into the crooks of their arms.

That could be you someday.

CAFETERIA: Ah, the cafeteria. Eating lunch is perhaps the scariest part of a high school student's life. It's the only part of the day that is completely free of structure—no one is in charge. When no adult is in charge, the potential for chaos—anarchy, even—is greater. This is why all the good movies about high school feature scenes in the cafeteria. Remember the "lunchtime poll" in *Heathers*? Well, your cafeteria is a bit different. For one thing, unlike a public-school cafeteria, which is big enough for you to hide in, the private-school cafeteria is teeny tiny. It's hard to sit alone. And it's hard not to be noticed if you do. I know one girl who used to go to the library during lunch and do her homework. I don't know if or when she ever ate. The thing is, I do not recommend this. You need to eat.

I bet you thought I was going to say to forgo lunch altogether. To never be seen eating anything. Now, now—there is absolutely no reason to go all Olsen twin. There's no need to pig out, either, but why not live a little? Mom and Dad already paid for it.

You still have to pay for stuff like lunch and books, even though you're on scholarship. When I started, Mom and Dad asked if I could bring my lunch, like I had always done, and the school said no. Everyone is supposed to eat the same thing. At the same time. Some girls will only eat saltines. Or a few pieces of lettuce. Some jocks will gorge themselves. Ignore them.

Lunch is, above all, a social activity. Eating is secondary. If you miss lunch, you will be like the person who uses a box with "No Photo Available" as their senior yearbook picture. And not in an ironic way. Seriously, no one will know who you are—or remember you. You will be Invisible Girl. You should sit with your class, even if no one invites you or you don't like them. Just grit your teeth and do it and smile and nod at the inane conversation and soon you will start to get to know the different personalities and figure out who is actually worth pursuing as a friend. Lunchtime hanging out is different than class or practice hanging out. If you skip it you will miss out on the inside jokes and the gossip and the invitations—which are usually casual, by the way, but when you hear them secondhand they never seem that way, they always seem as if you are being left out. But you're not. If you want to be a part of things, you can. It really is up to you. Most kids—boys especially—are passive. You have to take the initiative. Not everyone will respond, but you will know the ones who do are worth it.

In some cases, it is better to sit alone rather than with uncool people. If you sit at a table with uncool people, even if you are not technically sitting *with* them, you will be grouped with them, just for sitting near them. And it will be hard to shake the label. Sometimes the loner/rebel rep is preferable. You have to make the call, depending on the options in front of you.

Everyone complains about the food. You should, too, even as you're cleaning your plate. It's way better than what Mom gives us at home.

DANCE STUDIO: The Hiltons and Muffys tend to take dance as their art. They like all the mirrors.

DECK: The underclassmen tend to hang out here. The deck is a new part of the school and is seen as too nouveau for those of us who were there before it was built. But I'm sure your class won't have a problem with it. The upperclassmen prefer the back gardens and the hill (Senior Slope). Grass is preferable to wood, I find.

FACULTY LOUNGE: This mysterious and magical place is off-limits to students, except when you have to drop something off in one of the teachers' mailboxes. The door is always propped open, and it's fun to peer in and get a glimpse of the teachers off duty. I found the hanging mugs intriguing. Who belonged to which mug? VIRGINIA IS FOR LOVERS, I'D RATHER BE FISHING, #1 MOM. I had my suspicions.

FIELDS: Off-limits during school hours, except to the science teacher who used to take his foul-tempered dog for long walks here and let it run free. The fresh air didn't seem to help. I'm surprised it came back. The fields are also known for the "four-field run"—the pre- or postpractice words we all dread to hear.

FRONT HALL: Essentially the foyer of a mansion, which it was at one time. Rug, fireplace, big winding staircase, dog. Like the house in *The Sound of Music*. I thought we should line up on the stairs and sing "So Long, Farewell" to the guests gathered below.

The lowly hang out and start their homework here while waiting for rides home. Generally sophomores, freshmen, and the odd lame upperclassman.

GYM: I think it is technically known as the field house, but what exactly is a field house, anyway? It was always dead during the day. The off-the-grids go back behind the gym to smoke. Since the structure is windowless and off the beaten path, they aren't visible unless someone comes around the corner and surprises them.

HEADMASTER'S HOUSE: I mentioned earlier that the headmaster lives on campus. It's part of the deal with being headmaster. But no one has ever seen the inside of that house. His son is not allowed to have friends over, which doesn't matter, because he doesn't have any friends.

INFIRMARY: Well, the school doesn't have an infirmary or a nurse, but there is an ancient room on the second floor of the old wing. It has a cot where people can lie down if they feel bad, and it has a toilet. The cot is in the back, behind one of those old-fashioned screens I'm sure you've seen in old movies about hospitals. One day, Daisy Chilton felt sick after an assembly about global warming and the dean told her to go lie down until her mother got there. But Mr. Chips, who had made a habit out of using that bathroom because no one ever actually uses the room as an infirmary (and who was frankly too lazy to walk downstairs), was unaware that there was anyone lying on the cot. Well, you can imagine the rest.

LIBRARY: Hawkingville. Don't be seen here! If you are, be sure to talk loudly so you can get the librarian to throw you out. If you get thrown out enough times you can get banned for life. Which is fine with you. You don't need the library. You don't care!

LOCKER ROOMS: In the entire time I was at Plumstead, only one person ever took a shower in these showers. And she kept her clothes on. (She was a little crazy.) Until then, I wasn't sure they even worked. They haven't been renovated since the seventies, when they were built.

The senior girls have their own little separate locker area away from everyone else. They will walk around in their underwear and not care.

MAILBOXES: There are obviously no student mailboxes in public school. You can expect to receive notes, papers, handouts, tests, and messages here. Sometimes you might receive candy or fun things from your team captain or Secret Santa or some class fund-raiser.

Your mailbox (Petersen) is close to the floor, which has its advantages. (Few people are willing to bend down to try to sneak a peek at what's inside.) The disadvantage is that people have an overhead view of your butt when you're bent over to pull something out and they are walking down the stairs at the same time.

It's fun to receive real mail in a mailbox rather than an e-mail or an IM or a text. You never know what to expect.

"Five words: overhead view of your butt."
"Thanks, Bess. Got it the first time."

PARKING LOT: It gets full pretty fast, so get there early for a good space—or any space at all. Oh, I forgot—you'll never be driving!

POOL: The school has an outdoor pool in the back, but we're not allowed to use it. It's only for the summer-camp kids. It's always there, fenced in, taunting you, especially in May, when it gets warm. Last year right before graduation, some senior jocks drove to the school at night, scaled the fence, and went skinny-dipping. The cops came.

SNACK BAR: The snack bar gets sort of disgusting. There is definitely a certain kind of person who hangs out there. You'll find out. You'd think it would be cool but for some reason it's not. It became a refuge for the uncool early on, I think because the old guy who works there played favorites and some people got in with him, and then they felt empowered and took over the space. It's like how you discover a cool store or clothing label and part of the reason it's cool is because no one else has discovered it yet. But then you start wearing your outfit, and people ask you where you got it and you tell them, and then suddenly your discovery is popular and you don't even want to wear that outfit anymore because now it's not special. The snack bar is like that. It's not even worth going to anymore.

"Snack bar! Mother Teresa has a vending machine in the cafeteria. But I know one thing we have that you don't—a chapel! We also have a statue of Mary on the lawn. Does that count as sculpture?"

"Uh, I'm not sure."

"Apparently it gets toilet-papered a lot during football season."

42

EUPHORBIAS
[ACADEMICS]

Plumstead has tons of requirements, so you don't have too many options as far as choosing classes is concerned. And of course you're going to want to take a bunch of APs—that's not really negotiable.

You will actually be better prepared than the other kids. You've already had a language, and algebra, and the school will want to put you in advanced classes, with sophomores and dumb juniors. Resist. Stay with the freshmen, in freshman classes. If you don't, you won't get to know them, and you will be left out. That's what happened to me. I was in classes with sophomores and juniors, and the only other ninth grader was this girl named Jennifer Lee. All the ninth-grade idiot boys called her Bruce—you know, after Bruce Lee. I hated those boys. One day, one of them called me on the phone. He said he was with his two idiot friends and he was calling to tell me that one of them liked me. I hung up. All our phone numbers are listed in the Face Book, which I thought was stupid. Precisely for this reason.

COOL CLASSES: English seminars, Art History, French, Modern Dance, Calc (actually becomes cool again at this level because so few people make it—it's like climbing Everest or something).

UNCOOL CLASSES: Chemistry in the Community, AGT Math, Latin, European History, Spanish, Electronic Music.

COMMENCEMENT: Unlike at public school, where only the graduating seniors are expected to attend, all students at Plumstead must get dressed up and attend commencement. Some underclassmen will receive awards, which is weird, since it takes away from the seniors' day and their parents and families couldn't care less about you.

There's a private-school story making the rounds that at one school (not Plumstead) a kid actually sent fake letters out to parents, announcing that their children had won awards and inviting them to attend commencement. So a bunch of parents showed up and were really confused when their kids didn't receive any awards. They caught the guy who did it and he got in trouble—but not as much as you'd think. Just suspended.

COMMUNITY SERVICE REQUIREMENT: Private schools instituted a community service requirement a few years ago, to try to give back, blah

blah, and now before you can graduate you have to fulfill a certain number of hours. Do it early, and take advantage of group events the school sets up. You really don't want to spend your spring break senior year volunteering.

STUDY HALL: Required for first semester. You need to get good grades to get out of it for second semester, so make sure you do. It's either study hall or a free period. The losers are stuck in there for a second semester. Don't be one of them. You want your free period. Although I suppose it is one way to bond with some of your classmates. . . .

SUMMER READING TEST: It's a real thing. Take it seriously. Usually you have a week to finish reading once school starts, but every so often you get a new English teacher who wants to make a point that they mean business and they will give you the test on the first day of school. And technically you have no excuse. You can usually get away without reading the optional reading, but read the required one.

Knowing you, you will read more than the assigned amount. There's no need to publicize this. If the teacher asks on the test you can write your list in, but don't volunteer it. The teacher might decide to make an example of you, which will not go over well with the other kids, who either rented the movies or read the Cliff's Notes.

The latest trend seems to be that the entire school reads one book together and then when school starts they break you up into little discussion groups. Just like Oprah's book club.

"Do you have to do community service at Mother Teresa?"

"Are you kidding? I think I have to do like three times the hours you do. That's all they care about."

"Let's hope they don't make you sell chocolate bars."

"Very funny."

"You know I'm good for a couple milk with almonds."

BLUE OR BLACK FRUITS
[SPORTS]

In private school, you must do a sport for all three seasons, until senior year, when you can knock it down to two. So what happens to the kids who are bad at sports? They get kicked out. No, I'm just kidding. But they probably shouldn't bother attending Plumstead. There are options, of course: dance, theater (in the winter), being a team manager. And some kids get special permission to do an outside activity, like volunteer work, instead.

Most sports have three teams: varsity, junior varsity (JV), and thirds. Thirds is for the freshmen, but instead of calling it the freshman team they call it thirds because there is always some hapless sophomore (or junior, even) who gets stuck on it. Don't be that person.

FALL
GOLD

FIELD HOCKEY: Hiltons. There's nothing cuter for fall than a little field hockey skirt.
FOOTBALL: Jocks. Jackets.

SILVER

SOCCER: Okay for Normals.
CROSS-COUNTRY: Okay for boys, but not for girls.

BRONZE

FALL OUTDOOR PROGRAM: How to live/survive in the woods, rock climbing, and hiking for the off-the-grids/hippies/bad athletes who are against competition and violence. Definitely not cool.

WINTER
GOLD

ICE HOCKEY: Cool, especially for girls. (Private school has a girls' league.)

SILVER

BASKETBALL: Okay for jock boys, but the Muffys and Hiltons play ice hockey.

SKIING/SNOWBOARDING: Everyone wants to be the next Flying Tomato. Or at least get a nickname.

BRONZE

WINTER OUTDOOR PROGRAM: Even this beats fencing.

VOLLEYBALL: No.

FENCING: Worse than volleyball.

SPRING
GOLD

LACROSSE: The only choice. How else can you put one of those LAX stickers on your car?

SILVER

TENNIS: Okay, but it's cooler to play at the club during the summer rather than at school.

SAILING: Same as tennis—better done on your own time.

BASEBALL: It's not lacrosse.

BRONZE

SPRING OUTDOOR PROGRAM: The seasons may change, but its status remains the same.

SOFTBALL: Don't even think about it.

ATHLETIC BANQUET: This probably won't happen to you, but if you think you might win Most Improved Player, figure out a way to skip it. Getting MIP means one thing: that you sucked at the beginning of the season. And you are barely passable now. If you were good, you'd win MVP or Coach's Award or something else. If you truly can't get out of it, act nonchalant and uninterested, as if they called the wrong name and you are just going up to accept the award on behalf of someone who couldn't be there.

"Ha! This happened to Claire! She won Most Improved. She was so embarrassed. But then she put it on display on the mantel. When people came

over and asked about it she would say that our parents had put it there."

"I hope she dusted it herself."

HOOPER DAY: Hooper is Plumstead's fake athletic rival, essentially for the benefit of being able to have a day, called Hooper Day, with a cup. Or something similarly silver-plated. Hooper is a private school in Connecticut and I don't really know anything about it. We only hear about it on this one day. Plumstead/Hooper is not like Harvard/Yale or Yankees/Red Sox, where the rivalry is organic and long-standing. No, the school tells us Hooper is our rival, so every other year we go there on a long bus ride and on the opposite years they travel to us. It only happens in the fall, for some reason, and it honestly feels the same as any other game. Nothing special, except that if we win this game we get a cup. But there is no talk of going to steal their goat mascot or anything like that. For one thing, no one would even know how to get there.

MUSICAL: There is always a guy shortage.

TEAM MANAGER: If you pick this option it looks like you're not good enough to make varsity. Or you think you can be the coach.

"Sports are not required at Mother Teresa. Only prayer."

"That's a relief."

"Hey! I thought we had put the thrown-bat incident of sixth grade behind us."

"It's behind *us*, but the ump's knee might disagree."

NEUROTOXIC MUSHROOMS, VEILED, WITH FREE GILLS [ACTIVITIES]

There aren't as many activities as you'd think. There are actually more at the public school, where there are more kids. And at Plumstead everyone has to play a sport, so there's not as much time left over for other things. But it's important to join at least one of these clubs if you want to get into an acceptable college.

ASTRONOMY CLUB: I think most of the Hawkings are in this club for the telescopes.

COLLEGE BOWL: More Hawkings.

CYCLING CLUB: Everyone thinks they're the next Lance Armstrong.

ENVIRONMENTAL AWARENESS CLUB: They're trying to get Al Gore to come speak.

EVENTS COMMITTEE: Hiltons love to throw a good event, as long as it's about them and their "vision."

GERMAN CLUB: But the school doesn't offer German.

LINCOLN-DOUGLAS DEBATE CLUB (LD): Young Republican preps.

LIT MAG: Artsy wannabes.

MARTIAL ARTS CLUB: I think they meet secretly.

MATH TEAM: Still more geeks.

MEDITATION CLUB: A sophomore transfer started this "club." I left my sweater behind in Spanish one day and when I went back to get it they were "meeting"—sitting around in a circle smoking incense. I didn't even know incense could be smoked, but I left quickly. Freaks.

NEWSPAPER: The same Normals who do student council and yearbook. The newspaper is becoming obsolete, of course, but there is a popular gossip column ("The Owl") and a humorous advice column ("Ask Plummy").

PHILOSOPHY CLUB: What is the point of this club?

RESPONSIBLE CITIZENSHIP CLUB: What a joke. One of the jocks who got caught breaking into the pool was the president.

SCIENCE OLYMPIAD: All together now: "Hawkings."

STUDENT COUNCIL: The Normal kids try to get involved and make a difference. It's cute.

YEARBOOK: Why bother? No one's going to look at it after the first year of college anyway.

"What clubs was Claire in?"
"Like, all of these!"
"Didn't she . . ."
"Start the Philosophy, Environmental Awareness, and Martial Arts clubs? Yes. For her college applications."
"I thought it was because she had just seen *Rushmore*."

DEADLY MUSHROOMS RESEMBLING MORELS

[ASSEMBLIES]

Private schools love to get everyone together in one room. Yawn.

KINDS: Reasons for an assembly can range from a performance to a lecture. We've sat through student dance and holiday concerts, short plays, and debates. One kid spent his summer in Prague and gave a memorable and humorous PowerPoint presentation featuring a dead dog. I'm not sure why it was so funny. One girl came back from a semester in Scotland with a barely intelligible Scottish accent. Her presentation was not as well received.

RULES:

1. The first rule of assemblies is that there are always assemblies. At least once a week. For everything.
2. They are mandatory, but no one takes attendance.
3. Find your friends immediately or make a plan to meet beforehand so you are never stuck sitting alone or with people you don't know, or lame people or teachers. Best to sit in the back—you don't want to be picked as a volunteer. And *never*

actively volunteer. One year we had a sex ed assembly and Señora Froot Loop had the bad luck of sitting in the front row. (A bit too eager, if you ask me.) And of course, the sex ed person picked her for help in illustrating how strong condoms are, and before you knew it, Señora Froot Loop had the condom on her head. It was an unfortunate and embarrassing experience for everyone.

4. It's not cool to receive an award at the end-of-the-year awards assembly, so try not to do anything that would merit it. (It's always the same people anyway.)

5. Even if you enjoyed something at a particular assembly, never admit it.

"Somehow I don't think we're going to be having the sex ed assembly at Mother Teresa."

"No, probably not."

SUBTROPICAL SHRUBS
[BREAKS]

Private school has a different schedule than public school. We start later and end earlier in the year and we have more days off. We are above the law. It's annoying if your sibling (you) goes to a different school with a different schedule because then your family can't go on vacation unless one kid gets taken out of school. There were definitely parents who would take their kids out early or bring them back late so they could go on vacation. The school frowns on it, but those families didn't care.

If you want to survive private-school breaks, the best thing you can do is to learn how to ski or snowboard. I wish Mom and Dad were sporty parents. We really missed out. Other kids I know started skiing when they were two. Their parents just strapped the skis on and sent them down the hill. And that's how they learned. It's the best way, you know. At that age you're pretty low to the ground.

Lots of the kids ski every weekend. Their families have condos in places like Sunday River, Stowe, and Sugarbush. They have the stickers (MAD RIVER GLEN: SKI IT IF YOU CAN) on their cars and the North Face jackets to prove it.

And if you don't know how to ski, then you won't be able to go when your new friend invites you to her Sunday River condo for the weekend or on the student ski trip that your crush is going on.

Of course, Mom and Dad will go on and on about how expensive skiing is and how they can't afford to have you start now. Dad will tell his stickball story about how when he was in high school all they needed for a game was a broomstick and a ball made out of tape and they were good for hours. Just so you know, I've already given Mom and Dad the medal data on the U.S. Olympic Snowboard Team. I don't think they were convinced I was Olympic material.

Spring break poses a different problem. You will never get to go anywhere for spring break, but there will always be at least one blond Hilton or Muffy who comes back from one of the islands all brown, with her hair braided in beaded cornrows. She will leave them in as long as she can. Occasionally there are school-sponsored trips. Usually because a teacher wants to go somewhere and figures out a way to do it in the name of scholarship. Mom and Dad have always deemed these trips too expensive. But you wouldn't want to go to Cuba with Señora Froot Loop anyway. You'd never make it back.

Public school only gives you one week off at a time (one in February and one in April). Private school gives you two weeks in a row off in March instead. It's cruel, really. Everyone knows the re-adjustment period is much harder after two weeks. Around the middle of that second week, you really get into a groove, your freedom kicks in, you feel like Ferris Bueller on his day off. You begin to convince yourself that this non–high school existence is your real life and that you never have to go back. Oh, the humanity.

"You know what this means, don't you?"
"What?"
"We aren't on the same vacation schedule!"
"Well, we have summers. And Christmas vaca-tion." I was trying to be pragmatic.
"Great. But who am I going to go skiing with?" Bess smiled.

GILLED MUSHROOMS CAUSING SWEATING, TEARS, AND SALIVATION

[SOCIAL LIFE]

CURFEW: Mom and Dad are pretty lax about curfew. The state driving laws for people under eighteen come with a built-in curfew anyway. Don't brag too much about our parents being easy—you don't want people to think we come from some hippie house or something, or that we are such goody-goodies that our parents actually trust us.

DANCES: Private-school dances are never like what you see in movies or on TV. There will never ever be a choreographed dance number at one of your dances or proms. It was a nice part of *She's All That*, but it just ain't gonna happen. The only choreography will be in the musical, if they do *Grease* and keep the prom scene. But they would never do *Grease*—it's too mainstream, for one thing, and you need too many guys.

Don't overdress for a dance. Don't dance unless other people in your class do. And remember, hardly anyone slow dances anymore. This isn't the fifties.

DATING: Most likely you will not want to date one of the boys in your ninth-grade class. There will be fewer than five who are acceptable. And of those five, one will be "going out" with someone seriously, one will be a player, and the other three will not know their asses (or yours) from their elbows. Which leaves upperclassmen. You will have a crush on a senior, as will most of the other ninth-grade girls. There will only be one who is crush-worthy, and everyone will covet him, and he will only date a fellow senior.

Beware of the slumming senior. He will not really like you for you, he will just be unable to get anywhere with anyone his own age, which is sad, really, and he will try with a freshman because he assumes you are young and naive. So don't be young and naive! If you read this, you have no excuse.

But let's be honest. There isn't really that much dating in high school anymore. It's not like in Mom and Dad's day. And Plumstead is so small that there aren't even enough eligible guys to choose from. At Plumstead, there will be like one or two serious couples who go out for almost all four years of high school and have sex. Then there will be everybody else. Some people fool around at parties and throw around phrases like "friends with benefits," but don't be fooled. High school kids—especially boys—talk a good game, but most of them have as much (or as little) experience as you.

Oh, and don't worry. You may be taller than your male classmates now, but they'll grow.

FRIENDS FROM OTHER SCHOOLS: Your junior high friendships won't last long. It's hard to keep in touch with people you don't see every day, especially when they don't know what or who you are talking about! The same goes for boyfriends from other schools. Unless, of course, they go to an all-boys school.

> **Bess hit me in the shoulder. "Hey! This is about us. She knows I'm not going to Plumstead."**
>
> **"This is not going to happen to us. We'll talk at night and tell each other everything, just like always."**
>
> **"Are you sure?"**
>
> **"Positive."**

MALL: Never be seen shopping with Mom and/or Dad. If you are at the mall with them and find yourself in a crisis situation (someone from school is coming toward you), ditch them immediately. Either turn around and walk in the opposite direction or quickly duck into whatever store is closest, as long as it's not the Discovery Channel Store or Build-A-Bear. It is better to be seen with Mom and/or Dad than to be seen *allegedly* building a teddy bear. If the parent ditch is successful, meet up at the car later. Just tell them you got lost.

MOVIES: Attending the movie itself isn't that important. It's about seeing and being seen before and after the movie. It's about who you run into. (Actually, *all* events in high school are like that.) Of course, running into the dean of students at the artsy theater's annual midnight screening of *sex, lies, and videotape* is more than a little embarrassing.

PARTIES: Oh, the high school party. First of all, it's never as crazy as they make it out to be. Teenagers aren't as imaginative as the people in Hollywood think we are. Furthermore, don't expect to attend one party and suddenly have all the social barriers come crashing down, *Can't Hardly Wait* style. Kids aren't any different at parties than they are at school. All the groups will remain in place. You will not suddenly find yourself best friends with the head Hilton and dating the head jock just because you were under the same parentless roof one Saturday night.

Also, it's not cool to throw a party. Do not fall into the trap of thinking that throwing a party is the road to instant popularity. It isn't. First of all, our house is not big (or ritzy) enough. Second of all, the one thing that's actually accurate in those movies about high school is that the kid who throws the party never has a good time. In fact, she usually ends up calling the cops herself to clear the house out. And when all is said and done, most of the kids aren't even grateful to the party thrower. They don't say thank you. They don't help clean up. They don't treat her any nicer at school. They couldn't care less about her. They've used her for one night, and the next week they'll move on to whoever is hosting that weekend's party. Live and learn, sis. Live and learn.

PROM: There is really no place for a freshman at the senior prom. It's not about you. It's for the seniors, and the senior girls will resent you for taking a senior boy out of the running to either ask or be asked by one of them. There are never enough boys to go around. If you go, that will leave some senior girl having to ask a sophomore boy. A sophomore boy with one arm, who isn't able to slow dance (obviously) and will only care about being at the after party. Yes, slow dancing *is* acceptable at the prom.

I'm getting ahead of myself, but when it's time to go to the prom, the best option, if you aren't going out with anybody (ha), is to go by yourself. You will have a much better time. Trust me on this. You will understand—and thank me—later.

Remember, real life begins in college. At least, that's what the admissions people said.

"I don't want to wait until college for real life to begin."

"She's just trying to make us feel better about our lack of boyfriends."

"Don't remind me. Not all of us are like Claire."

"I felt kind of bad for Rob. He was not expecting it at all. I think he thought they would date all through college and then get married."

"Has he ever met your sister?"

"She, of course, was more interested in starting college unattached. Which makes sense, actually. Rob's going to the University of Chicago. It's not like they were going to be close. She'll have a new boyfriend by the end of September."

"Maybe your sister's next book should be a field guide to dating."

FRUITS OR SEEDS, BRIGHT RED/ORANGE
[SCHOOL SPIRIT]

School spirit: yes or no? Well, that depends. Plumstead is such a small school that it's hard to get too excited about it. School spirit is either all or nothing. If everyone is pepped up over some game and you're not, you'll stand out. But if you are the only one who shows up at morning meeting with your face painted? Well, you won't be able to live it down.

CHEERLEADERS: Plumstead doesn't have cheerleaders. But it has cheerleader types.

FUND-RAISERS: Whenever one of the classes sponsors a fund-raiser where you send your friends a chocolate lollipop or candy cane, send one to yourself, unsigned. Just in case. You will feel better—what if you hadn't gotten any?—and it looks good. Leave it in your mailbox all day so people will see. And hope that you receive more than just that one.

The most popular fund-raiser is Jeans Day, where you pay a certain amount to be able to wear a pair of jeans to school for the day. Even some of the teachers participate. (Although not all of them look good in jeans.)

GAMES: Hardly anyone watches games, since almost everyone plays a sport and has a game at the same time. Sometimes boys hockey and basketball draws some spectators, usually underclassmen with crushes.

PENNY DRIVE: I am vehemently opposed to the penny drive as fund-raiser. Why should I give my hard-saved pennies, picked up off the sidewalk for good luck, to the sophomore class just because they are lazy and failed to raise any money? Is that my fault? Besides, why should I donate money to another class? So they can have a prom two years from now, when I will be long gone? No thanks.

SECRET SANTA:

Upside: My Secret Santa once put coal (along with an assortment of candy) in my mailbox, which I found oddly appealing. I knew who it was—he was so obvious about it—but he never revealed himself to me, even during the party at which he was supposed to do so. (He walked by me ten times instead.) Downside: I once got the dean of students. If that happens to you, try to trade with someone.

The other downside is that even though there's a spending limit, it's generally expected that people will go over it and give the kind of gift that one would be happy to receive oneself. Well, I always had the bad luck of being picked by the person who passes off a crappy regift as their Secret Santa gift, after I went out and got a gift certificate to Sephora or something nice like that. (Not for the dean of students, of course. He got a crappy ornament.)

"Finally! Some information I can use. I will never sign up for Secret Santa."

"Yeah, but are you really going to send a candy cane to yourself?"

"I might have to! It's not like you can come over to Plumstead to send me one."

"I don't even *like* candy canes."

PARASITIC SHRUBS; MISTLETOES
[TRADITIONS AND WEIRD PRIVATE-SCHOOL STUFF]

Private schools like to have their traditions and special quirks. And—just between you and me—some of them are downright wacky.

BANDS: The school always has a few bands/singing groups going. You will be subjected to their musical stylings at various assemblies and events.

ROCK BAND (ALMOST FAMOUS): One long-haired guy on lead guitar, girl on drums. They play covers and some unintelligible original tunes.

COMBO (STACY'S MOM): Snobby band-geek types do Muzak covers of *TRL* faves.

GUY AND A GUITAR (JOHN HAIR): Angsty indie power pop straight out of the pages of his blog.

GIRL GROUP (FATE'S ORPHAN): One Muffy, one hippie, and one Hilton. Three *American Idol* auditions.

"Where is Simon Cowell when you need him?"
"Obviously not at Plumstead!"

BREAKFAST AT NIGHT (OR BAN): I'm not sure when this tradition started, but it was actually a lot of fun. It involved staying at the school on a weeknight for dinner, which was actually breakfast. As in breakfast food. They had everything—eggs, pancakes, French toast, bacon, hash browns, bagels, fruit. And then while we were eating breakfast people would get up and perform—sing, play an instrument, read something, juggle—and the school bands would play. Sort of like *America's Got Talent* but without Regis or the Hoff. One year this goth girl did a dead-on imitation of the dean of students. People were rolling around on the floor laughing and he was smiling but seemed embarrassed. And one year the Latin teacher got up and said he was going to do impressions. "This is my impression of President Bush," he said, and then instead of mimicking him, he said, "Well, I think the President . . . ," etc. etc. etc., and told us what he thought of him. You know, his impression. Some people didn't get it.

But I don't know if you will even have Breakfast at Night, because this year this freshman kid did a rather suggestive striptease to "Gold Digger." He took his shirt off, swung it around his head a few times, and flung it at Madame Beaucoup, the French teacher. He got a standing ovation (including from

Madame) but the next day he was called to the dean of students' office. And that could be the end of BAN at Plumstead as we have known it. Someone started a petition to keep it going, but I don't know if it will help. It would be so sad if your class missed out.

"Catholic school definitely doesn't have BAN."
"Well, it sounds like Plumstead won't have BAN anymore, anyway."
"I wish I could have seen that dance."

CLASS JOBS: Each class has a cleanup job, to which two students are assigned each week. They make you work to go to Plumstead, even though your parents are paying thousands of dollars.

CLASS TRIPS: Private schools insist on sending each class on an Outward Bound–type class trip. I think they are secretly trying to get rid of a few of us, as they are obsessed with sending us out in extreme conditions so that we can learn so-called survival techniques. In case we ever want to be contestants on *Survivor* or *The Amazing Race*.

The ninth-grade class trip is, thankfully, only a one-day thing. Not an overnight. I guess they don't think you're ready for that yet. Well, try to be sick this day anyway. I'm serious. Nothing good comes of it.

If you do get stuck going, try to get in a group with nice people. And don't make a spectacle of yourself by saying you are afraid of heights or whatever. Just suck it up. Take a deep breath and let them strap you in for the ropes courses and figure that if you fall and die, Mom and Dad can sue the school for a lot of money. The outcome won't be entirely bad.

If any of the midget ninth-grade boys makes a crack about how they are going to get you over that wall thing, threaten to drop them. Loudly.

The only interesting thing about the ninth-grade class trip is the opportunity it provides to see some of the male teachers', uh, packages, accentuated by the safety harnesses. It will be the talk of the day. You might regret missing it.

You won't regret missing when one of the Hiltons is the only person to do the highest ropes course and one of the skaters keeps uttering "What a woman!" over and over again.

My year, before we even got to the ropes courses, we were all waiting at school for the bus that would take us there. At that point, people were still getting to know each other. This one girl, who was nothing special in my opinion and had these large dead Barbie eyes that revealed that very little was going on inside, was the last to arrive. When she did, every single other ninth-grade girl except my friend and me surrounded her car, calling out as one, "Heather! Heather's here! Heather!" I'd never seen anything like it. They surrounded her the way the other contestants surround Miss America when she's crowned. She was in a convertible, and she almost could have been sitting on top of the backseat with a bouquet of roses in her arms. They swarmed to her like bees to honey. It was disgusting.

"Another reason to be grateful you're not going to Plumstead with me: you won't be left for dead on the summit of some ice cap in New Hampshire."

"Sorry to break it to you, And, but I don't think there are any ice caps in New Hampshire."

"Oh."

"COMMUNITY": Plumstead loves to refer to itself as the "Plumstead community." It's not a school; it's a community. Everyone is part of it. When bad things happen, they affect not one person but the entire "Plumstead community." It'll make you gag after a few weeks.

DOGS: People in private school love their dogs. There was always at least one dog roaming around. I know you're allergic, but I don't think they'll bother you. They just laze about the front hall and roam outside. You don't have to roll around on the rug in the front hall, but I don't recommend telling people you hate dogs or anything. Pretend you love them, too. There will be one dog that everyone loves and one dog that everyone hates. One faculty dog will inevitably be named after a Grateful Dead song.

One faculty member (okay, a history teacher) my sophomore year had a scary dog named Churchill. He used to bark and run at people when they walked by the science office, which was where he stayed during the day, and the Hiltons would always scream. Everyone referred to Churchill as Hitler, but only behind the history teacher's back. She was the sweetest person, and no one could understand why her dog was so mean. Eventually Churchill/Hitler scared one too many students and parents began to complain, so he was driven from the school. Banned. That faculty member only lasted one year. I'd be willing to bet that being stuck in the science wing was the source of the dog's anger.

DRESS CODE: Private school has a dress code! No jeans, no sweatpants, no T-shirts. Shoes must be worn. (Not sure why they have to specify this—I suppose some of the kids don't *want* service.) It sucks, but, as I said earlier, every year at least one class sponsors Jeans Day as a fund-raiser, and almost everyone participates. Hey, at least there's not a uniform.

Oh, and if you don't comply with the code, they might ask you to change or send you home. And if they ask you to change, it might be into something you find in Pandora's Box (see next page), which you really won't want to do. But as of April Fool's Day every year, Bermuda shorts are acceptable. So on April 1, regardless of whether there is still snow on the ground (which there sometimes is), almost the entire school shows up wearing shorts.

FIVE-YEAR PLAN: Some of the football players and even some of the kids who transfer in from public school end up repeating a year, meaning that their parents pay for five years. I don't understand it.

JUST SAY NO: Once a year you will be required to attend a "Just Say No" to drugs workshop that won't really teach you anything you don't already know. It never really had an impact, as far as I could tell.

MASCOT: You know how normal schools are called the Tigers or the Eagles or the Panthers or something like that? Something that works in sports? Well, at Plumstead, we are the Owls. You know, because owls are smart. Wise. They are supposed to represent knowledge. But they don't exactly inspire fear in athletic opponents. It's embarrassing. The other teams hoot at us. They say things like "Hey, thought you only came out at night!" and "How many licks does it take?" And they call us Harry Potters—"Where's your pet owl, Harry?"—and Hooters, naturally. One football player couldn't take it—he ended up transferring. Now he's a Ram. The good thing is that some concerned parents and alums finally went to the school and complained. The newly formed Athletic Team Identity Committee is supposed to study the matter this year.

PANDORA'S BOX: It's really just a plain old cardboard box that's used for lost and found. But of course everything has to be a literary reference! They keep it in the front office and make a big show of "opening" it if you need to look for something. Try not to lose anything—it gets pretty nasty.

RECESS: At first it was embarrassing. We're in high school and we need a daily milk-and-cookies break? Please. For a public-school kid, it was unthinkable. But after a few weeks, you get used to it. And learn to love it. In fact, it quickly becomes your favorite part of the day. It's not as stressful as lunch in terms of where to sit, because it's so casual. You can just grab your snack and go or hang out briefly and eat.

Flo (the lunch lady) hands out the cookies. (Two each.) They are different every day. Not homemade, but it doesn't matter. If you butter her up, she might even give you a second helping. She loved me—you can try telling her you're my sister. (But don't use that with anyone else.) Recess really is the best thing about Plumstead. Don't ever skip or miss it, because you will be sad when it's gone.

RIDICULOUS NICKNAMES: Prepare yourself for the ridiculous nicknames now so you don't laugh. I'm sure you've heard some of them from my time: Taffy, Jazzy, Junior, Bunny. Things you would name your dog.

"Remember when Claire tried to get us to give her a nickname?"

"Yes! Pete! From Petersen, our last name. She was in her Madonna phase and she wanted to do that English thing where girls have boys' nicknames."

"You were the only one who went along with it. I just thought it was stupid. You are a good sister."

"I try."

WELLINGTON DAY: Wellington Day is named after Wellington, the beloved dog of Plumstead's first headmaster. It's sort of like Groundhog Day. Once a year, during second semester, just when things are starting to get stressful and hectic, the headmaster brings his dog, Skip (Wellington is long gone), out for his morning walk. If the dog does his business in a certain secret spot, the headmaster declares Wellington Day, which means we get the next day off! An all-school, unscheduled holiday. But he doesn't have to, and if things aren't going well, either at school or with Skip, he won't give us Wellington Day that year.

It's sort of like getting a snow day in public school. The euphoric feeling is the same, but with snow days you always have to make them up in June, at the end of the school year. They are never free.

Bess was rolling around on the floor laughing.

"Would you please get up?"

"Is this a joke? This has got to be made up."

"No, it's real. I remember Claire being home

for Wellington Day when I had to go to school. I was so mad."

"Maybe she was pulling a Ferris."

"What?"

"Maybe Claire just made up Wellington Day to trick your parents into thinking she had a day off."

"Knowing Claire, that's entirely possible."

"You'll find out soon enough. But if it is true, please don't rub it in."

COMPOSITES WITHOUT SHOWY RAY FLOWERS
[ONE LAST THING]

This is the most important thing. If you don't get a good picture taken on the first day of school for the Face Book, then just forget it. You are screwed. Don't bother showing up the next day. Transfer. That stupid Face Book is the Bible for the next nine months of your life. And you don't get another shot until the following year. Believe me, your year can pretty much be determined by the kind of Face Book picture you end up with. Sure, you say now that it doesn't matter to you, that you're not that shallow, but you'd be surprised. Everyone judges a book by its cover. Especially in high school!

So do not—I repeat, do not—screw up that photo. Because they will not let you do it again, and they certainly will not let you put another photo there instead.

Plus, it's not like those books are collected at the end of the year and destroyed. No, some people keep them for, like, ever. I still have all four of my books, and even the one from the year before, when I went for my interview. It has seniors I've never even met in it. That picture is the only memory most of the seniors will have of you. Try to make it a good one.

What you don't want is some skanky MySpace picture. Trust me. Just keep it simple. Normal. Please. If you don't, change your last name.

"Hahaha. Some skanky MySpace picture!"

I was starting to get a little annoyed with Bess. "It's like Claire's never met me before."

Bess composed herself. "I don't think Mother T has a school directory. Or if we do, there are no pictures."

"I wish *we* didn't have pictures. It's impossible to be anonymous in such a small school."

"That's the point. I'm hungry."

I looked at my watch. It was already noon and we hadn't moved from the kitchen table. If I had gone with Claire, I would have been drinking lemonade and eating cookies at some welcome reception. Or maybe we would have gone out to lunch in town.

"Should we do pizza now or wait for dinner?"

"Now."

I got the number from the fridge.

"Cheese okay?"

"Perfect."

"Cheesy bread?"

"Yes!"

Claire always made us get a veggie topping, to

make it more healthy. Now that she was gone I could do things my way. I picked up the phone to call, but there was someone on it.

"Hello?"

"So, what do you think?"

"About what?"

Bess looked at me like I was nuts. "Claire!" I mouthed, pointing to the phone, which hadn't rung.

"Who are you talking to?"

"No one. You."

"Is Bess there? Are you letting her read the book?"

"What do you think?" Claire was silent. I jumped at my chance.

"Sorry, gotta go!" I hung up. Claire hadn't said not to show the book to anyone, but it didn't seem like the right time to get into it. I picked up the phone again. Dial tone. Whew. I dialed the pizza place and ordered.

Bess waited until I hung up for a second time. "What did she want? Why is she calling you so much on her first day of college? Shouldn't she be orienting?"

"She wanted to know what I thought of the book. And she didn't sound so happy about the fact that you might be reading it, too."

"Who cares? It's not like it's that helpful to me

or anything. There are some funny bits. But what I don't get is this: I thought your sister loved Plumstead. She sure acted like it, anyway."

I had been wondering the same thing. "Apparently she didn't love it as much as we thought."

"Maybe she thought pretending was the only way to survive. Maybe she wants to spare you."

"Spare me? From what? High school, like death, is inevitable. One way or the other, it's gotta happen."

"Except for the homeschoolers! Maybe your parents will let you be homeschooled. There are always a ton of those kids in the national spelling bee. . . ."

"But I don't want to be homeschooled. Until today I was actually looking forward to high school. Why does she always have to ruin everything?"

"Your sister is only one person. This is only her opinion. We need to forget about Claire."

The doorbell and the phone rang at the same time. Thirty minutes or less! I ran to answer the phone and handed Bess the pizza money.

"Are you alone?"

It was my sister. Again.

"Sort of. What is *up* with you?"

"There's another chapter. Under your mattress. It's just for you."

Bess was on her way back to the kitchen.

"What? Why is it just for me?" But Claire had hung up. Another chapter? Should I tell Bess about it?

"Who was that?"

"Who do you think? Let's eat."

We sat back down at the kitchen table and dug in. Reading about high school had made me hungry. I decided not to mention what Claire had said, for now.

"What I don't get is why she would insist that I play field hockey, when she knows I love soccer. And I know for a fact that if we ever went on vacation to one of those places like Jamaica, she would get those braids done. And we both know that she did not know how to ski."

"Remember the time she went skiing on that school trip and went on a black diamond trail and had to take her skis off and walk down? Everything about Claire needs to be taken with a big grain of salt. Including this so-called field guide. But I have to admit I'm feeling a little jealous." Bess took a bite of pizza. "Now *I* want to go to Plumstead. Mother T does not have dance class. Or mailboxes. And it may be a Catholic school, but everyone has locks on their book lockers."

"Maybe Claire just didn't get how good she

had it. The minute she got to Plumstead she seemed to forget she had ever stepped foot in a public school."

"Well, you're not Claire."

"Neither are you."

"Right, and she's obviously delusional. All that stuff about not looking like you tried so hard—what is she talking about? She never ever once went to school without looking like she had spent two hours getting ready, which she had."

Bess laughed. "Yeah! How many times did we have to wait for her to get ready before she could drop us off somewhere? We've spent half our lives waiting for your sister."

"Like that *Waiting for Guffman* movie."

"But he never showed up."

"What's worse? Being late? Or never showing up at all?"

"My mom always says better late than never."

"Late people always say that. It makes them feel better.

"Well, Claire isn't here to make us late anymore!"

"Yeah, but we have no ride, either."

We were both quiet.

The phone rang again.

We looked at each other.

"Hello?"

"How's everything going, Andie?"

"Mom," I mouthed to Bess. "Fine, Mom. I'm just going through my closet to see what I have for school."

"Good. Dad and I will call again from the road."

"Okay. Love you. Bye."

I hung up as quickly as I could.

"Your closet?" Bess looked confused.

"I didn't want her to know you were here, in case Claire was there. And I don't think they need to know about the book."

"Probably not. Of course, Claire probably couldn't resist telling them about it, so she could score some extra big-sister points."

"You are so right." I pushed the pizza box out of the way and opened the book to Part Two.

"Ready?"

"Ready."

part two
VENOMOUS ANIMALS

These are the kinds of kids you
might meet in high school.

FOUR YEARS OF HIGH SCHOOL. WILL YOU SPEND
THEM COOL WITH US? OR AS A SOCIAL LOSER OUT-
CAST WITH HER? YOU DECIDE.
—PAIGE, *Degrassi: The Next Generation*

MAMMALS
[YOUR FELLOW CLASSMATES: AN OVERVIEW]

* 3 football-player jocks
* 1 slut
* 1 gay boy who doesn't know it yet
* 1 crazy as in cuckoo girl
* 1 legacy son
* 6 geeky short guys
* 1 class clown
* 1 weirdo
* 2 popped-collar preps
* 2 hippie girls
* 2 skater dudes
* 2 juvie boys
* 8 nondescript girls
* 1 Mafia princess
* 1 undeserving queen bee
* 2 mean girls
* 1 androgynous outcast
* 1 scary smart guy
* 1 old-money snob
* 1 black girl
* 1 Indian boy
* 1 goth girl
* your 1 friend
* you

SCORPIONS/SPIDERS/CENTIPEDES
[SOPHOMORES/JUNIORS/SENIORS]

While most of your social interactions will take place within your freshman class, you still go to school with three other grades, and like it or not, they will be a part of your daily life. In some cases you will be in the same classes or on the same sports teams. Here's what you need to know.

SOPHOMORES: As a freshman girl, the people you need to worry about the most are the sophomores. They are cocky. They made it through their first year, they are back, and they are no longer freshmen. That is enough for them to walk around as if they rule the place. Even the unpopular sophomores are snotty and treat the freshmen like shit. Unlike the juniors, they don't have to worry about college yet, and because you are here, they no longer have to worry about the seniors picking on them. Yes, sophomores are the ones to watch out for. They have no fear. They will try to date freshmen girls. They will try to make varsity. They *will* sting you.

JUNIORS: Juniors are being pulled in all directions. They are too busy studying for SATs and meeting with the college counselor and joining every activity in a last-minute attempt to get involved and improve their college applications. They are freaked out and stuck in a web of their own making. As long as you don't get caught in it, you won't have to worry about them.

SENIORS: You will know all their names and everything about them, but don't flatter yourself: they will have no idea who the hell you are. And they won't care.

Plus, the senior advisor they assign you will be nice to you the day you meet her but will ignore you for the rest of the year.

Remember *The Lion King*? "The Circle of Life"? Well, high school is its own circle. Every year the senior boys conveniently forget what it felt like to be the lowest on the totem pole and haze the freshman boys. Three years later, when the freshmen are finally seniors, they do exactly the same thing to the new kids. In this way, the cycle continues. And once the seniors are safely into the college of (hopefully) their choice, they can sing "Hakuna Matata" and really mean it.

CATERPILLARS
[HAWKINGS]

SIMILAR SPECIES: Geeks. Nerds. Brainiacs. Eggheads.

EXAMPLES: Doogie Howser, MD. Screech. Urkel. Napoleon Dynamite.

BEHAVIOR: Hand constantly in air to answer questions.

IDENTIFICATION: AP Calculus book

AS SEEN IN: *Freaks and Geeks. Head of the Class.*

HABITAT: Library. Science wing. Computer lab. A/V booth.

NOTE: Hawkings are actually sweet one-on-one.

DESCRIPTION: The trick to being smart in high school is to be smart without actually letting anyone know. You need to be nonchalant about it. Shrug as if you couldn't possibly explain how you just pulled that A or that correct answer out of your butt. Never let them see you sweat. I don't care if you win the Nobel Prize in Physics, it's not cool to brag. The true geeks, of course, don't know better. They beam happily when the headmaster announces their latest Science League conquest. They loudly proclaim their love for George Lucas, NASA, and *Battlestar Galactica* without a second thought. They dress up as Anakin for Halloween. So don't begrudge them their calculators and MIT early admissions—it's all they have. And they need it.

Mom claims that Dad actually used to be a Hawking. She says Hawkings are like caterpillars. They might be furry and gross and you might want to step on them, but if you wait around long enough they turn into beautiful butterflies.

I doubt it.

DIAMONDBACK RATTLESNAKES
[JOCKS]

SIMILAR SPECIES: Puck/helmet heads. Basketball robots.

EXAMPLES: Slater. Luke from *The OC*.

BEHAVIOR: Hand constantly in air to high-five someone. Mouth constantly open for championship eating. Team jacket constantly on.

IDENTIFICATION: Baseball hat. Smirk.

AS SEEN IN: *Heathers. Can't Hardly Wait. High School Musical.*

HABITAT: Gym. Field. Rink.

NOTE: In most cases, their rattle is worse than their bite.

DESCRIPTION: Rattlesnakes have rattles, which alert you to their dangerous approach. Most high school students do not. If only they did; life would be so much easier. Sometimes the ones you need to be wary of are the ones who don't make a sound. They seem safe enough, but they strike when you least expect it.

However, the jocks' rattle (like most everything about them) is obvious. You can hear them coming a mile away. Their cars, their mouths, their shoes, their hair—everything about them is loud. Plus, they travel in a pack.

I'd like to be able to say that all the clichés aren't true. That you will find that one special well-rounded jock like the basketball player in *High School Musical* who will star with you in the school play. But I can't. A football player is a football player is a football player. You will not be discovering an Einstein or a Wordsworth in this group. Don't be deceived when they take dance to fulfill their art requirement. They are just making fun of it, like everything else.

BEES
[THEATER PEOPLE]

SIMILAR SPECIES: Play people. Drama geeks.

EXAMPLES: Sharpay and Ryan.

BEHAVIOR: Will break into song at any given moment, for any reason.

IDENTIFICATION: Jazz hands. "Vision." Big finish.

AS SEEN IN: *High School Musical.*

HABITAT: Theater. In line to see *Avenue Q* for the millionth time.

NOTE: When they talk about their "instrument," they mean their voice.

DESCRIPTION: Theater people spend entire lunch periods:

* Reciting lines from *Spelling Bee* or *Avenue Q* or *Wicked* or whatever the new Broadway show is.
* Discussing the merits of Chita Rivera's Velma vs. Bebe Neuwirth's vs. Catherine Zeta-Jones's.
* Tackling important questions like whether the cast of *Rent* was too old for the movie. Or whether Hugh Jackman is straight.

You will never have any idea what they are talking about. They swarm around with their inside jokes and like to make fun of and talk over each other and do that annoying "snap" thing and sometimes you just aren't in the mood. They can be sarcastic, which can be refreshing at times but can also sting if the sarcasm's directed at you.

Theater people have their own special gossip, which is pretty boring if you don't really care if Sally should get the female lead this year because she's been in the musical since freshman year and she's a senior even though the new junior transfer is a *much* better singer.

WASPS
[MUFFYS]

SIMILAR SPECIES: Preps. Rich kids. Snobs. Richie Riches. Trustafarians.

EXAMPLES: Summer Roberts. Blair Warner. Lisa Turtle.

BEHAVIOR: Referring—nasally—to their father as "Daddy."

IDENTIFICATION: Stupid dog. Stupid nickname.

AS SEEN IN: *Cruel Intentions. Beverly Hills, 90210. Pretty in Pink.*

HABITAT: Expensive foreign cars. Islands. Their own wing at home.

NOTE: There will always be some Muffy who never has any money "with her" and hangs out in the snack bar all day trying to mooch. Don't give in.

DESCRIPTION: Since Plumstead is a private school, most of the kids actually fit into this category. But there are some who are more obvious about it than others. BTW, male Muffys are known as "Biffs." This category also includes legacies, those kids who have older brothers and/or sisters at the school or whose parents went there. The legacy children are usually nightmares and their parents are completely clueless. The legacy siblings aren't as bad—there's often at least *one* down-to-earth member of the family.

There is a subspecies of this category known as trustafarians, which are rich preppy kids who are usually also stoners. Dreadlocks optional. Basically they are just bored. Their dads are saving lives as doctors. Their moms are saving lives as inner-city literacy volunteers. And somehow their parents have forgotten about their own kid.

But there's no need to feel sorry for the Muffys and Biffs. After all, they don't feel sorry for you.

COTTONMOUTHS
[OFF-THE-GRIDS]

SIMILAR SPECIES: Freaks. Weirdos. Basket cases.

EXAMPLES: Allison from *The Breakfast Club*. J.D. from *Heathers*.

BEHAVIOR: Nonverbal communication. (And I don't mean ASL.)

IDENTIFICATION: Muscle car. Fake accent. Analyst.

AS SEEN IN: *Dazed and Confused. Freaks and Geeks.*

HABITAT: The great outdoors. Parking lot. Boiler room.

NOTE: Always keep at least one arm's length away.

DESCRIPTION: There aren't that many weirdos at Plumstead. It's a private school, after all; they don't have to let them in. But there are at least a couple in each grade. They make things interesting. When I was a sophomore, there was this one senior who started using a cane. Not like an old person's cane, but a Fred-Astaire-from-the-old-movies cane. It might have worked if he'd added the hat and the tails, but he wore khakis and polo shirts. There are scary weirdos, too. One kid would only respond with "All in all you're just another brick in the wall" anytime anyone asked him anything or said hello. In the cafeteria he would say, "If you don't eat your meat, you can't have any pudding!" I guess he was hungry.

SHREWS AND GILA MONSTERS
[HILTONS]

SIMILAR SPECIES: Mean girls. The Plastics. Heathers. Pretties. Princesses. Popular people. Cheerleaders. Beautiful people.

EXAMPLES: Heathers. Cher from *Clueless*. Kelly from *Saved by the Bell*.

BEHAVIOR: Frequent hair whipping, color/outfit coordinating, not eating.

IDENTIFICATION: Long hair. Evil eye. Little dog.

AS SEEN IN: *Heathers. Mean Girls. Popular. Clueless.*

HABITAT: Mall. Bathroom.

NOTE: Dig below the surface and they're just like everybody else.

DESCRIPTION: Oh, the Hiltons. They look perfect, even at sports practice. They have all the boys wrapped around their fingers, even the leftover boys, who would never stand a chance with them. But the Hiltons aren't really happy. It's all a carefully constructed façade.

I know, I know. It's hard to remember when you're in the thick of it, watching them strut around the school as if they own it, seeing everyone, even the faculty, fall all over themselves to get on their good sides. Trust me: the best way to deal with these girls is to ignore them. Pretend they don't exist. They can't stand that. They will do anything to get attention. Which is why they are always switching boyfriends and being mean. They want people to talk about them. They want to always be the center of things. But when you add up all the non-Hiltons, you will realize that you are in the majority. The Hiltons are so superexclusive that their numbers are actually quite small—never more than five or six per grade. If all the other groups joined together, the Hiltons would be completely outnumbered.

"So what is your sister? A Hilton or a Muffy?"

"She's probably more of a Hilton, but in some ways she's her own category. I mean, she used to tell me that she would wear her hair a certain way and then the next day half the girls in her class would show up with the same hair. She used to play around and do stupid things just to see if other people would copy her."

"Would they?"

"Yes! It was crazy."

NONVENOMOUS INSECTS
[NORMALS]

SIMILAR SPECIES: Normal Kids. "All-around" people.

EXAMPLES: Angela Chase. Joey Potter. Veronica Mars. Eric and Donna. You.

BEHAVIOR: Hanging out. Laughing. Studying. Having fun.

IDENTIFICATION: Book bag. Homework.

AS SEEN IN: *Dawson's Creek. That '70s Show. My So-Called Life.*

HABITAT: School. Home. Practice. Movies. Mall. Friends' houses.

NOTE: Regardless of what I've said before, the truth is, almost everyone falls into this group.

DESCRIPTION: This should make you happy. Yes, there are normal kids at this school. In fact, most of the kids are b-o-r-i-n-g. Nothing special or distinguishing about them. They don't bite, they aren't poisonous, they are just as confused and insecure as you are.

That's right, you don't have to wear Manolos or Lacoste or dye your hair turquoise or invent something or make the Olympic soccer team to fit in. You can just be yourself. Gag. (Although in your case you might want to work on your wardrobe. And your hair. And your personality.)

FLOWERS INCONSPICUOUS IN UPPER AXILS OR TERMINAL CLUSTERS

[LEFTOVERS]

SIMILAR SPECIES: Everyone else. People without a country. The Others.

DESCRIPTION: It's hard if you don't really fit into any of the groups. Even some of the rich kids—the ones who aren't pretty or good at sports—end up here. The school is so small that the Leftovers end up forming their own group, even though they are brought together not by mutual interests but by the fact that they don't belong anywhere else. And you know how people feel about leftovers: no one likes them the next day.

Leftovers usually include the following:

CLASS CLOWN: Oh, the Class Clown. Making the world laugh but crying on the inside.

FOREIGN EXCHANGE STUDENT: There's often one token Foreign Exchange Student, like Fez on

That '70s Show. In real life, the FES is nice and sweet but too different to be fully embraced by the popular kids. Unlike Pedro, he or she will never become class president. FESs have an accent, and their clothes and haircut are always just a little off. They stay on the fringes. And let's be honest, who the FES ends up living with makes a big difference, too. There aren't too many popular kids who would agree to let a kid from another country come live with them and then take him or her under their wing. So the FES often ends up living with a fellow Leftover, and well, that doesn't help either party.

GOTHS: Black doesn't really fit into the preppy palette, so there aren't too many goths. Maybe two or three in the whole school. They hang together sullenly, all pasty faces and dyed-black hair.

HIPPIES: I suppose it's refreshing to have a few people diverge from the A & F uniform, but these people—with their flowy skirts and dirty hair—annoy me. Especially the vegan one with the SUV.

NONWHITE KIDS: There are a few, but overall, prep school is like *Friends*. Why were there no black friends? Not even hanging out at Central Perk? The show was set in New York City! A picture of one of the black students will appear in every single catalog and piece of literature about the school. I found it frustrating, but the black girl in my class said it didn't bother her. She just laughed about it. (And don't get me started on those idiotic guys who *pretend* to be black.)

SCHOLARSHIP KIDS: You can't really tell who the scholarship kids are. It's not like they have to work in the cafeteria or anything. But you can sort of figure it out based on who doesn't get a car for their sixteenth birthday.

> **"Wasn't your sister a scholarship kid?"**
> **"Yup. How quickly they forget."**

SKATERS: The handful of skater dudes wear baggy pants that are always about to fall off and walk around looking like they've received one too many blows to the head. As far as I know, none of them has ever tried to have a pizza delivered to class.

SLUTS: I don't condone the use of the word, of course, but every class has one. She's usually a very nice person with some issues. She's the kind of girl who doesn't really hang out with other girls, and I think she's lonely. She seems to thrive on the attention she gets from boys, but they never end up becoming her boyfriends. Some boys will mistakenly think that you are a slut, too, if you befriend her, which is not a reason not to befriend her. It's just an example of how stupid boys are. Oh, and there are male sluts, too, by the way.

STONERS: It's hard to be a true stoner in private school, since, unlike in public school, you can get kicked out. But there are a few who achieve this status—I don't understand how. *Everyone*—even the dogs—knew that this one kid in my class was *always* stoned. Did the teachers just not see it? Or did they choose not to?

STUDENT COUNCIL: It's hard to know what these people do, exactly, or why they want to do it. There are student council people and non–student council people. You'll figure out the difference. The president of the student council is always a senior, and depending on who it is, he or she can really influence the vibe and tone of the whole school year. Last year, the Karl Rove Club (now defunct) *allegedly* engaged in some ballot-box stuffing, but nobody did anything about it and we were stuck with a real idiot. (I won't name names.)

TECH SUPPORT: This kid is the go-to guy for all your audiovisual needs. He is the only one who knows how to do anything, so he essentially lives in the booth in the auditorium, running the lights and sound for every assembly, show, concert, and class. In fact, he is often called out of his own classes to help some Luddite teacher in need.

TOMS: These kids have thousands of friends on MySpace but none in real life. It's sad.

BLISTER BEETLES
[FACULTY]

SIMILAR SPECIES: [Unprintable]

EXAMPLES: Mr. Moore from *Head of the Class.* Guy from *Ferris Bueller's Day Off.* Mrs. Garrett.

BEHAVIOR: Adult. Supposedly.

IDENTIFICATION: Shit car. Public radio tote bag. Elbow Patches. Sensible shoes.

AS SEEN IN: *Boston Public. Saved by the Bell. Welcome Back, Kotter.*

HABITAT: Classroom.

There are as many different types of faculty as there are students. Here are a few examples:

OF AMBIGUOUS SEXUAL ORIENTATION: At least one teacher—usually from the French department—falls into this category, and everyone obsesses over whether he or she is gay.

CREEPY: There is always the one mad-scientist-creepy teacher who is too much of a close-talker, says things that are just on the other side of appropriate, and gets a little too much pleasure out of frog dissection day in bio. Harmless, but you don't want to get stuck with this guy alone or even get involved in conversation with him.

FORMER STUDENT: In private school, there is a phenomenon wherein a former student returns to the school to teach. I suppose it is possible it happens in public school, too, but I never noticed it. You don't really want these teachers, because they don't know what they're doing yet. They haven't learned how to be teachers. Plus, when you think about it, they are only like four years older than the seniors. Ick. When I was there, a guy came back, fresh out of college. He was twenty-two and all the senior girls had crushes on him.

OLD: The old teachers fall into two categories. There are the ones who have kept up and are beloved and respected by all. And then there are the obsolete ones, still teaching their original syllabi from the first class they ever taught.

IN OVER THEIR HEAD: This happened to one of my Spanish teachers. It was his first time teaching, and he couldn't control the class, and everyone knew it and took advantage. I felt sorry for him, and one day he asked if he could talk to me and told me he was having problems with the class and asked if I could help—maybe talk to people, try to encourage them to cooperate. I said I would see what I could do, but I felt awkward. It was a strange position to be in. So I didn't do anything. I even tried to ignore his friendly overtures in public. I cared more about what my classmates thought of me than what he thought. But now, telling you about it, I feel guilty. I should have tried to help. He left after that one year.

YOUNG: The young faculty people can go either way. Sometimes they are cool, and respectful, and treat us like equals. They are hip, and young enough to remember what high school is like. It helps if they like music and movies and let us talk about stuff besides schoolwork in class every so often. But then there are the ones who try too hard. They care too much about being cool, about what we think of them. They want to be loved and to fit in with us, to make up for not fitting in when they were students, maybe, and of course we can smell that sort of thing a mile away. And it's sad.

"Now, this information is actually helpful. I'm sure I'll have teachers like this at Mother Teresa."
"Plus the nuns."
"There aren't that many anymore."

OTHER PEOPLE YOU WILL NEED TO DEAL WITH

ADMISSIONS GUY: Independently wealthy. Has spoiled dog.

CHEF: Everyone hates the food, but once a year the headmaster asks Chef Bob to come out from the kitchen, which he does, in his chef's hat, and the headmaster thanks him for a "delicious meal" and everyone claps.

COLLEGE ADVISOR: Useless. Tells everyone to go to her alma mater.

DEAN OF STUDENTS: The heavy. Disciplinarian, but he has a soft side. I was sent to him once, after telling this annoying Jock where to go during art history. Well, we both went to the dean, but although he tried to hide it, the dean was more amused than mad. He didn't do anything.

GROUNDS CREW: The nicest guys at the school. (Like Hagrid!) Most of the kids ignore them, so they remember and appreciate the ones who are friendly.

HEADMASTER: Figurehead. Doesn't seem to have anything better to do than memorize the directory because he knows every single kid by name and will greet you by name every single time he sees you. Of course, he has the unfortunate initials B.J.—for Ben Jonson—which is how everyone always refers to him.

LUNCH LADY: Flo, the keeper of the cookies.

PARENTS/ALUMS/TRUSTEES: You will get to know some of these adults because they are around all the time. Apparently they don't work, because they appear to devote all their time to the school. They have money and nicknames like Kicky and their children don't tend to be all that popular.

SCHOOL SECRETARY: The head secretary in the front office, Pearl, knows all. She's the one really running things. Make friends with her and you'll be set.

THE FOOD CHAIN

TOP:
HILTONS
JOCKS
MUFFYS

MIDDLE:
NORMALS
THEATER PEOPLE

BOTTOM:
HAWKINGS
OFF-THE-GRIDS
LEFTOVERS

The Hiltons get along with the Jocks, the Muffys, and in select cases, the Normals and the Theater People.

The Jocks get along with the Hiltons.

The Muffys get along with the Hiltons, and in select cases, the Normals and the Theater People.

The Normals get along with the Theater People, and in select cases, the Muffys and the Hiltons.

The Theater People get along with the Normals.

The Hawkings, the Off-the-Grids, and the Leftovers are on their own.

ANTS
[STRENGTH IN NUMBERS]

Most high school students ornament themselves. They attempt to create an identity with their clothes, hair, accessories, friends. But many high school students should not be judged by their markings. While the diamond pattern on a rattlesnake should always be taken seriously, sometimes teenagers get confused about their marks and find themselves in the wrong category.

I guess I'm trying to say that these labels are not ideal. And I don't think anybody actually likes them. And yet we all keep using them anyway. Sister to sister, the important thing to remember is that everyone—Hawkings, Jocks, Theater People, Muffys, Off-the-Grids, Hiltons, Normals, and Leftovers—is insecure. Everyone. Insecure. Equally.

If there was some United Nations of high school or something and every high school student had a vote and agreed to stop putting people into these little groups, that would be one thing. But it will never actually happen. So how do you rise above it? At the risk of getting all *High School Musical* on you, the key is to define yourself not by one thing and one thing only but by many. The Hawkings get labeled Hawkings because they don't do anything else to distinguish themselves. If you do a bunch of different things—soccer, College Bowl, lit mag, calc—then you will confuse people and they won't know what category to put you in. That's the goal. (The other goal is to not do all the same things I did. Then you will just get compared to me all the time.) So who's a good example of this? Oprah. Yeah, a Mom example, but it's late and I need to pack for school. Angelina Jolie, maybe, but not quite yet. (And she's going to have to stop adopting.) Mandy Moore or Lindsay Lohan? Please. Oprah has her talk show. Then she has her magazine. She produces movies and Broadway shows. She acts. She reads. She gives money away and builds schools in Africa. She defies categorization.

One advantage of a small school like Plumstead is that it does allow for a certain amount of travel between groups, though it takes a certain kind of person to pull that off. I don't wholeheartedly recommend it.

Finally, if you're going to be stepped on, it is important to have at least one ally. Even if it's a Leftover. I never thought I'd say this, but in high school, it's better than being alone.

EXTRA CREDIT

BOOKS

Forget required summer reading. These are the books to read before you get there:

1. *Angus, Thongs and Full-Frontal Snogging,* by Louise Rennison: This book from England will make you laugh out loud and wish Plumstead had a uniform. Perfect to get you in a good mood after a bad day.
2. *Boy Meets Boy,* by David Levithan: Plumstead doesn't even have a Gay-Straight Alliance, which is all the more reason to read this special book about a special high school.
3. *The Boyfriend List,* by E. Lockhart: The funny and inspiring trials and tribulations of Ruby Oliver, Seattle prep-school sophomore.
4. *The Catcher in the Rye,* by J. D. Salinger: This is one English-teacher fave that actually lives up to the hype.
5. *Gossip Girl,* by Cecily von Ziegesar: The first one is the best!
6. *Prep,* by Curtis Sittenfeld: Oh, I forgot—you read this one already.
7. *Teen Angst? Naaah . . . ,* by Ned Vizzini: One boy's humorous experiences at ultracompetitive (you have to take an exam to get in) Stuyvesant High School in New York City.

8. *Boy Proof*, by Cecil Castellucci: The main character of this sweet book loves science fiction movies and lives in Los Angeles.
9. *Harry Potter and the Scorcerer's Stone*, by J. K. Rowling: Everyone will pretend not to care when the next movie comes out but they will go see it opening weekend.
10. *Lord of the Flies*, by William Golding: Probably best not to find yourself on a deserted island with your classmates.
11. *The Outsiders*, by S. E. Hinton: Before there were Jocks and Preps there were Greasers and Socs.

"Isn't there a girl in *Gossip Girl* named Claire?"

"No! It's Blair—not Claire! And she is *much* worse than my sister."

MOVIES AND TELEVISION SHOWS

You and Bess should check these out if you haven't
seen them already.

1. *10 Things I Hate About You:* Sadly, most high
   school boys don't look like Heath Ledger.
2. *Buffy the Vampire Slayer* (TV): Be grateful your
   high school just *feels* like hell.
3. *Can't Buy Me Love:* Dr. McDreamy!
4. *Can't Hardly Wait:* Sure, four years of high school
   and it all comes down to one party.
5. *Clueless:* Read *Emma*, watch *Clueless*, write a
   paper comparing and contrasting, get an A.
6. *Dawson's Creek* (TV): Remember when you and
   Bess set up a ladder so she could climb in your
   window and Dad put the ladder away and Bess
   got stuck on the roof?
7. *Ferris Bueller's Day Off:* Real high school boys
   aren't this cool. Save Ferris!
8. *High School Musical:* Make it stop.
9. *Freaks and Geeks* (TV): All the good shows about
   high school get cancelled.
10. *Mean Girls:* One word: "Plastics."
11. *My So-Called Life* (TV): Two words: "Jordan
    Catalano."
12. *Pretty in Pink:* Classic. But don't get any smart
    ideas about making your own prom dress.

13. *She's All That:* That girl was beautiful. She didn't need a makeover. And certainly not from Freddie Prinze, Jr.
14. *Sixteen Candles:* In real life that guy never would have shown up at the end.
15. *Veronica Mars* (TV): No one messes with Veronica. When you find yourself in a difficult situation just ask: What Would Veronica Do?

"What do all these movies have in common?"

"They're all about high school?"

"No, none of them are R-rated! What is her deal? Does your sister not realize we've seen everything already?"

"She knows. She's just trying to impress my parents."

"So what's missing? *Heathers*!"

"*The Breakfast Club*!"

"*Rushmore*?"

"Yes, definitely. Claire loves *Rushmore*."

"*American Pie*?"

"Yuck. No. I think we're done."

BACK-TO-SCHOOL SOUND TRACK

"WORD UP!"—Cameo

"ME AND JULIO DOWN BY THE SCHOOLYARD"
—Paul Simon

"WE'RE GOING TO BE FRIENDS"—The White Stripes

"SONG 2"—Blur

"WRAPPED UP IN BOOKS"—Belle & Sebastian

"FRIDAY I'M IN LOVE"—The Cure

"LOSER"—Beck

"BEVERLY HILLS"—Weezer

"DON'T ASK ME"—OK Go

"PUBLIC SERVICE ANNOUNCEMENT"—The Bravery

"ABC"—Jackson 5

"PIRANHAS ARE A VERY TRICKY SPECIES"—Mark
Mothersbaugh

"MMMBOP"—Hanson

"SOMEWHERE OVER THE RAINBOW"—Israel
Kamakawiwo'ole

"CORNER OF THE SKY"—*Pippin* soundtrack

"BREAKAWAY"—Kelly Clarkson

"SHINY HAPPY PEOPLE"—R.E.M.

"ACADEMY FIGHT SONG"—Mission of Burma

"FOR ONCE IN MY LIFE"—Stevie Wonder

"Pippin?"

* * *

"Well, your sister obviously did not have anything better to do this summer."

"It sure doesn't seem like it. But I never saw her working on this. She was hardly home all summer."

"I wonder how she'd feel if we wrote *her* a field guide to college?"

"She would not appreciate it. Not that we'd even know what to write."

"Oh, I can think of a few things. . . ."

The phone rang. It was either my parents or Claire.

"Hello?"

"Andie, I don't know what to do." Claire.

"About what?"

"Mom and Dad just left, and my room is all set up, and now I don't know what to do." I looked at Bess. She was never going to believe this.

"Well, let me consult your guide."

"Andie, that guide was for high school. Not college. There is no field guide to college. Believe me—I've checked."

"Where is your roommate?"

"She's hanging out in the hallway. There are a bunch of people just sitting on the floor out there."

"So go out there."

"And do what?"

"Sit down."

"But I don't know them!"

"Come on, Claire. You not only survived high school, you excelled at it. You ran Plumstead. College is nothing. And you're making a worse first impression sitting alone in your room than the one you're afraid I'm going to make." Bess raised her eyebrows at me.

I tried to make my best "you're never going to believe this" face back.

"So you did read it?"

"Every word. Bess, too."

"What did you guys think? Should I try to expand it? Maybe get an agent—"

I cut her off. "Why don't you get through your first day of college first?"

"Well, okay. I guess you're right. I garble you, Andie."

"What?"

"I miss you!"

"You do?"

"Of course. Don't you miss me?"

"Uh . . ."

Claire laughed.

"Claire?"

"Yeah?"

"Thanks."

"You too. Gotta go! Someone is knocking on my door!"

"Bye!" I turned toward the wall and hung up. I

was afraid I might start crying, and I didn't want Bess to see.

"What was that all about?"

"Sister stuff."

"Oh."

My parents would be home soon. I started to clean the pizza box and plates off the table. Bess was flipping through the guide.

"And?"

"Yeah?"

"What are you going to wear?"

"Where?"

"To school. On the first day. I've got my uniform. You need to plan."

"I haven't even thought about it. I better check with Claire."

After Bess left, I went to my room to get the secret chapter Claire had mentioned on the phone. I felt a little guilty, but I had known Claire longer, after all. If there was anything terribly important, I would fill Bess in later.

Bug Spray
For your eyes ONLY!

Hey, Andie.

Me again.

The truth is, there is no field guide to high school. I made it all up. One of the many annoying things about high school is that everyone just has to figure it out for themselves. And you and I are *so* different—what worked for me isn't necessarily going to work for you. But I've done my part—at least I can't blame myself.

If this field guide were *The OC*, this is when that annoying music would start playing and Ryan would ring the doorbell, and when Seth and Sandy and the mother (whatever her name is) opened it, Ryan would be standing there with a black eye but they would pull him inside and have a group hug while the music played and the screen faded.

The point is, you are going to be fine. You don't need a book. You don't need Bess. You don't even—ahem—need me. You're much cooler than I was at your age.

You know, I'm starting over too, just like you. And yes, even *I* worry. But you're lucky. Not only do you have a great friend, Bess, to share everything with, but you also have an older sister (me) to give you advice. There are days I wish *I* had me for me. But I'm happy to have you.

So here's a final piece of advice: don't talk about people behind their backs. Because you *will* get caught.

I closed the book. That Claire—she always had to get in the last word. Not this time! I heard a car pull into the driveway—Mom and Dad must be back. I quickly put the book under my mattress and blew my nose. I didn't want them to think I had been crying or anything. Claire would just love that.

Acknowledgments

Many thanks to my first and second cousins and their friends for answering all my questions about high school:

* Ashley Brady
* Michael J. Butts
* Andrew Craddock
* Meghan Dalton
* Molly Dalton
* Alessandra Fisher
* Kate Healey
* Amelia Ladd
* Mathias LeBlanc
* Kara McWade
* Deanna Moore
* Adam Nesti
* James O'Sullivan
* Maggie O'Sullivan
* Katherine Paquette
* Hayley Smith
* Moses Tran
* John Wall

Thanks also to Dutchy Smith, Helen Smith, Christine Titus, Gerry Titus, Lainey Titus, Ruthie Titus, Matt Walker, Coley Walsh, Debbie Walsh, Joseph Walsh, and Steven Walsh.

Special thanks to Suzy Capozzi, Angela Carlino, Colleen Fellingham, Rebecca Gudelis, Beverly Horowitz, Elizabeth Kaplan, and Tamar Schwartz.